*Beery*

# TALKIES

## GHOST STORIES *of* HAWAII

Created
by
*Roland Roy*

D1364065

ISLAND HERITAGE

# TALKIES
## Ghost Stories of Hawai'i

Created and illustrated by Roland Roy
Edited by Christine Flanagan

Published by
ISLAND HERITAGE
P U B L I S H I N G
99-880 Iwaena Street
Aiea, Hawaii 96701
(808) 487-7299
E-mail: hawaii4u@pixi.com

ISBN NO. 0-89610-304-8
First Edition, Second Printing - 2001

# DEDICATION

*To my wife, Toni, a wonderful schoolteacher,*
*and to my son, Gino, my faithful reader.*

# TALKIES
## Ghost Stories of Hawai'i

# TABLE OF CONTENTS

## - INTRODUCTION -
*vi*

## - STORIES -
The House for Rent

*1*

The Pali

*25*

The Obake

*39*

Nu'uanu Cemetery

*55*

Ni'ihau, The Last Banzai

*71*

## - ILLUSTRATIONS -
*Page iv, vii, viii, 24, 38, 54, and 70.*

# Introduction

## A note to parents and teachers

*Talkies-Ghost Stories of Hawaii* is an interactive reader designed for individuals or groups: schools, parties, clubs—anytime kids gather. They'll participate in reading through involvement.

Here's how it works: each person will volunteer for a part. The lead reader will be the narrator, or storyteller. Some can volunteer to take charge of sound effects («►EFX◄») to make the story exciting. *Talkies* will entice kids to see how a story develops. It's fun, but more importantly, it will reveal the fundamental components of a story: character, conflict, resolution. In the process, struggling readers will enjoy seeing a story come to life through participation.

While designed to entertain young readers, *Talkies* will also help them become better readers. My hope is that readers will delight in these stories, advance to higher levels of reading, and be inspired to create their own stories.

# About the Author...

**ROLAND ROY** is a Hawai'i-born artist and writer who has worked for CBS and MGM Studios in art direction, and holds numerous credits in advertising and magazine illustration. He has won awards in poetry and documentary film making (including the prestigious New York Film Award at the New York Film Festival) and his artwork has been shown in exhibitions across the country. He has also worked for the Honolulu Police Department.

Mr. Roy currently teaches at Moorpark College, California, and makes his home in Newbury Park, California.

# The House For Rent

## CHARACTERS

Storyteller

Papa Gouveia, *Owner of the house many years ago*
Mama Gouveia, *his wife*
Daughter Gouveia
Son Gouveia

Mr. Akau, *Renter of the house today*
Mrs. Akau, *his wife*
Akau, Jr., *his son*
Leilani Akau, *his daughter*

Mr. Liu, *Landlord*
Samoan 1
Samoan 2
Kahuna
Emilio, *the servant*

Ghosts: *Voices of children, warning voices*

## Special effects (EFX)

*Footsteps*
*Door slamming*
*Howling wind*
*Knock at door*

# STORYTELLER

There it was, perched high on a hill, staged like a craggy finger gesturing toward something evil. It overlooked the homes below, threatening strangers with its dark windows that resembled eyes searching for prey. It was one of the first houses here, people say, built for the very rich around the turn of the century. The house yearned to tell a tale or two just by the way it stood, staunch, mocking, gazing toward the ocean like a prison guard. It had a winding staircase starting from the one-car stone garage at the bottom that went all the way to the back of the house, to the kitchen. In the early days, the servants would climb these stairs every day after shopping at the markets in town. Once, people thought the house was elegant. It had high ceilings, custom stained glass windows and a handrail that surrounded the verandah. It is here that our story takes place. It is here that the past remains and still roams the premises.

Sometimes, while gazing at this house, a cold chill will bite you and leave you damp with sweat. You feel a slight panic, a need to escape. It is here that a perpetual "For Rent" sign has finally lured some unfortunate fools to the door. They don't know what once happened here.

But wait!

Let's not get hasty. No need to rush. Just listen
now to the past. The owners are sitting on the
verandah barking orders to their servants below.
Listen.

### PAPA GOUVEIA
(*angry*) Get those branches down.
C'mon, you lazy bums. After that,
clean the basement. There's a lot of
work to do. Get going!

### DAUGHTER GOUVEIA
(*agreeing*) Yes, Papa. They're just a
bunch of lazy bums.

### SON GOUVEIA
Hey, you, Japanese man! Go clean
the basement. Hurry up! You, too,
Filipino boy!

### MAMA GOUVEIA
Oh, let them be. They're up to their
necks in work. I'll do it. I can help.

### PAPA GOUVEIA
Mama, you betta stop! These people are like a bunch of goats. I pay
them. I'll tell them what to do.
Understand?

**MAMA GOUVEIA**
Yes, Papa.  You the boss.

**STORYTELLER**
That's the Gouveia family. Big shots that lived in
the house, high on a grassy knoll, looking down
on all the other people in the town as if they were
commoners. In their old country, they treated
people cruelly, with no feelings of remorse. The
Gouveias enjoyed the pain they inflicted, pushing
the knife of ridicule deep into people's souls. All
except Mama.

The Gouveia family was a breed of imports.
Locals called them *luna*, or boss. Some called
them "The Devils," wealthy Portuguese settling
down in a new land, Hawai'i, known then as the
"Jewel of the Pacific," or "Paradise."

The house was built in Nu'uanu Valley, a place of
tropical charm and beauty. The fragrance of
plumeria and ginger permeated the air like no
other place on earth. The red ginger pointed its
glory like hands in prayer to the Hawaiian gods.
Hawai'i now has some unwanted visitors.
Hawai'i has ways of dealing with tyrants. Hawai'i
has tricks of her own.

Now, let's go to the present day. It is fifty years
later. A family is eager to rent this "castle." They

are baffled by the low price. They are mesmerized by its size. New to Nuʻuanu Valley, they are oblivious to its history. But that's not important now. What's important is that they are here and the house is hungry for new souls. No one has lived here for years. The people of Nuʻuanu know its past: they've heard crashing glass in the middle of the night, seen the red glow in Daughter Gouveia's room on the second floor, heard voices echoing throughout the valley at midnight, crying for help.

### GHOSTS
(*children's voices*) Mama! Mama!
(*angry, low voices*) Go home. No come here.

### ((►EFX◄))
*Footsteps. Doors slam. Howling wind.*

### GHOSTS
(*baby voices crying and low warning voice*) Go home! You going die. You going *make*. Stay away! Everybody going *make* here. Run away!

**STORYTELLER**

But this new family hasn't heard the noises. They wait patiently next to the rent sign. As they look up at the house, Akau, Jr. spots a face in the window, staring at him. He grabs his mother's dress.

**AKAU, JR.**

Ma, ma! (*pointing*) He stay up there.

**MRS. AKAU**

Who stay up there? Where?

**AKAU, JR.**

Up there. Up there. The man!

**LEILANI**

(*joking*) Get ghost up there, that's why. I can play with ghost, you know. Good fun.

**AKAU, JR.**

Who asked you, 'uku?

**LEILANI**

You one 'uku! Mommy— Junior calling me names.

**STORYTELLER**

The Akau family stands and stares at the house, watching it's ever-changing moods, when an old Chinese man stumbles toward them, startling the family. It's Mr. Liu, the landlord. He has a worn leather briefcase with the rental agreement in it. Mr. Liu struggles to get the papers out of his brief-case, but his pants have no belt, and he must hold them up with one hand. He drops the papers. The kids giggle as Mr. Akau helps him.

**MR. AKAU**
Hey, you guys, be quiet. Old man, somebody die over here, or what?

**MRS. AKAU**
Yeah, somebody die, or what? Why you say cheap?

**MR. LIU**
No, nobody *make* for long time. Old house. Somebody got to *make* sometime. You going *make*, I going *make*...

**MR. AKAU**
Yeah, yeah, okay. How much the house?

**MR. LIU**

Three hundred dollar. Cheap, no?
Three hundred, 'nough.

**MRS. AKAU**

What's the deal, man? No more
electricity? No more oven, or what?

**MR. LIU**

Get. Get plenty. Free furniture, too.
Get everything inside. Go look.
Nice. Go see. Nice house, that.
Three hundred dollar. Cheap!

**MR. AKAU**

(*whispering to his wife*) Hey, ma. We
can save plenty *kālā*. If we no like
the place in six months, we can
move with plenty money saved up.

**MRS. AKAU**

Take the bugga. Hurry up.

**MR. AKAU**

Okay, okay, Mr. Liu. I'll take it, but I
want only a six-month lease, just to
be sure. Six months, all right?

**MR. LIU**

Sure, sure. Six months, okay. (*to himself*) If you last that long.

**STORYTELLER**

Mr. Liu takes the legal papers out right there, on the street. He doesn't want to go in the house. He reaches for his pen, lays the agreement on the hood of his car. He's nervous, hurrying before the Akaus change their mind. Suddenly, as Mr. Akau signs his signature, a freak crash of lightning and thunder is hurled above the valley as if warning, "Now I've got you!"

Mrs. Akau orders her troupe to get their things quickly and head for the house. Two Samoans are there to help with the heavier furniture.

**SAMOAN 1**

(scared) You gotta pay me for live here. I no kid you, brah. Spooky, man.

**SAMOAN 2**

You can say that again, Malu. I heard about this place, brah. Somebody's head went chop off. I wouldn't move here for nothing.

**SAMOAN 1**

Hurry up, then, Moke. Getting dark.
No more light in the house.

**SAMOAN 2**

Six o'clock already. Shake a leg,
Malu. Get cranking.

**STORYTELLER**

The two Samoans go to the back of a large pick-up and grab some large items. As they look up, gray billowing clouds hover over the house like large, thick hands. The Samoans hurry to unload the truck.

Mr. Liu runs away as a light drizzle blankets Nuʻuanu. He can't believe they took the house. He sits inside his car, out of breath, watching as the Akaus take their belongings up the staircase. They look like obedient pets walking into the mouth of the devil. Mr. Liu shuts his car door and leans forward to see the last person being devoured by the hungry house. He starts his car and laughs callously to himself.

**MR. LIU**

Take care, my little chickens. Hope
you last for six months. Good luck.

**STORYTELLER**
7:30 p.m. First night. Darkness settles in. The Akaus are groping, trying to put things away.

**MRS. AKAU**
Junior—Leilani! Go find the candles. I no can see nothing. Hurry up! Now! Somebody going get hurt.

**AKAU, JR.**
Hey, Leilani. Go find the candles, 'uku.

**LEILANI**
You one 'uku. Mommy! Junior making me cry again!

**AKAU, JR.**
Hey, shut up. You like beef, or what?

**《▶EFX◀》**
*Howling wind blows. Door slams.*

**AKAU, JR./LEILANI**
Mommmyyyy!

**MR. AKAU**

You broking my ears! Hey, Ma, I got
all the candles you need. Ooh, you
feel that cold wind?

**SAMOAN 1**

I wish I had one cold breeze. I
sweating like one pig over here.

**SAMOAN 2**

Yeah, Malu. Hurry up, brah. I like
split this place, man. I get chicken
skin already.

**STORYTELLER**

The Samoans are trying to move an old heavy
sofa from one room to another. They reach under
the sofa, hands grasping the legs as they lift.
Suddenly their hands slip and the sofa plummets
back to the floor—and moves back to its original
spot! They look at each other, eyes out of their
sockets, spooked.

**SAMOAN 1/SAMOAN 2**

Gotta go! See you guys later. No
need pay us. Take care, Mr. Akau.
A-looooo-ha!

## STORYTELLER

The front door crashes as the two large men scoot out of the house and down to their truck, not stopping to look back. What did the Samoans know about the house? Why so scared? Let's go back in time again, back to another day in the past with the Gouveia family.

Mr. Gouveia is yelling at his servants, as always, causing them to shiver with fear. He relishes his power. He often scares them, sometimes causing accidents that hurt them. One of his servants, a frail teenage Filipino boy, broke his leg so severely that he has a permanent limp. His name is Emilio. Today, Emilio is talking to a Hawaiian priest, a Kahuna. Emilio is telling the Kahuna how badly the servants are treated at the Gouveia's. The Kahuna, holding his sacred staff, listens carefully to Emilio. He turns and faces the evil house and raises his staff in defiance.

## KAHUNA

Why you no go see the police?
Emilio, he going hurt you bad. You
must not go back.

**EMILIO**

I have to go back. No more work
anywhere. I gotta help my family.

**KAHUNA**

Okay, let me go with you, then. I
can talk to him.

**EMILIO**

No, Kahuna, no! Don't come with
me. He going hurt me more.

**STORYTELLER**

Emilio limps inside to work. He is late and he'll
have to pay for it today. As he opens the kitchen
door, he can hear Mr. Gouveia barking orders to
the servants. Mr. Gouveia has started drinking
early and is especially unpleasant. Emilio tries to
be quiet as he creeps into his work clothes, but
Mr. Gouveia hears him enter.

**PAPA GOUVEIA**

Emilio! You late again, you cripple.
Where you went? Come here.

**EMILIO**

(*frightened*) So sorry, boss. My leg
get hard time come up the steps.

### STORYTELLER
Mr. Gouveia grabs Emilio's shirt, his devil face turning beet red.

### PAPA GOUVEIA
You nothing. You one goat! You
late again and I teach you—

### ((▶EFX◀))
*Knock at door.*

### STORYTELLER
Mr. Gouveia releases Emilio and stumbles over to the front door. There is the old Hawaiian Kahuna with his staff. Mr. Gouveia stares menacingly at the Kahuna. The Kahuna shows no fear. He looks straight into the animal eyes of Mr. Gouveia.

### PAPA GOUVEIA
Well, who you? What you want?

### EMILIO
Mr. Gouveia, that's the Kahuna, a
powerful priest. He is my dear
friend.

**STORYTELLER**

Mr. Gouveia grabs a nearby vase and throws it at Emilio. The vase crashes next to Emilio's head, shattering into broken pieces. Emilio loses his balance and falls to the floor. The Kahuna moves to help him. Mrs. Gouveia is shocked. Her children are screaming for their father to stop.

Just then, Mr. Gouveia grabs the sacred staff from the Kahuna and swings wildly at the Kahuna and Mrs. Gouveia. Mr. Gouveia slips as he swings the staff and grabs onto a tall antique clock for balance. The clock sways forward, then falls on top of the Kahuna and Mrs. Gouveia. They are crushed. In his last breath, the Kahuna speaks.

**KAHUNA**

You are a bad man. You can do
what you wish with me, but
behold, this house will be your
prison forever. Each of you will suf-
fer by my gods.

**PAPA GOUVEIA**

This is all an accident! An accident!
I... I...

*16*

**STORYTELLER**

Holding the Kahuna's sacred staff in his hands,
Mr. Gouveia, stunned, realizes what he has done.
Suddenly, his hands begin to burn—the Kahuna's
staff becomes alive with intense heat. Frightened,
he runs out to the verandah and heaves the sacred
staff into the dense brush below the house.

When the police arrive, they find Mr. Gouveia
dazed and muttering incoherently. The faces of
his children are blank with disbelief.

As the years pass, each of the Gouveia children
die a slow and painful death, feeling the powerful
curse of the Kahuna. The ghost of Mama Gouveia
still roams the house in search of her children.
She can't rest until she is released by the Kahuna.
Only the Kahuna can set her free.

Now do you see? This is the house where the
Akaus have settled, fifty years later.

**MRS. AKAU**
>(*impatient*) Junior, Leilani, get to
>bed. Now! And stop playing with
>the candles or we all going to burn
>down with the house. Junior!
>Leilani!

**JUNIOR/LEILANI**
Yes, Mommy.

**LEILANI**
Hey, leave the candle alone. *Okole.*

**AKAU, JR.**
You one *okole.* I no need light anyway. I brave.

**LEILANI**
Yeah, right. Banana.

**STORYTELLER**
Mr. Akau is in the living room putting things away. It's almost midnight, and he is tired. In one box, he finds a hand mirror, and when he looks in it, he sees another face. A woman crying. Mr. Akau drops the mirror in shock and the mirror crashes to the floor. The woman's cries echo through the house. Mr. Akau thinks he's crazy. He tries to yell for Mrs. Akau, but his voice is grounded in his throat. Then, he hears his children yelling. Upstairs, his wife screams when she sees the children. But Mr. Akau can't go to help. His legs are held to the ground by an unknown force. As he stands there, helpless, moving his arms to try and get loose, he curses the evil house.

Meanwhile, Mrs. Akau is terrified. In her bedroom, Leilani is being sucked into a mirror as Junior holds on tight to her body.

#### MRS. AKAU
(*frantic*) Who are you? What you doing? Let go of my daughter!

#### AKAU, JR.
(*crying*) Ma, I'm holding Leilani. Ma! Broke the mirror! Broke the mirror before Leilani get sucked in. Hurry!

#### STORYTELLER
The ghost appears in a blue whirling light, screaming and encircling the room, forcing the furniture to leave the ground. Mrs. Akau has fallen to the floor. She can't walk: the floor is moving, all the wooden boards slapping violently. The house is angry. Only Junior is able to hold on.

#### MRS. AKAU
Why my kids? Ghost, get your own kids. Leave my kids alone!

#### ((▶EFX◀))
*Doors slam.  Howling winds rise.*

**MRS. GOUVEIA (ghost)**
(*circling Mrs. Akau's children*) My
son. My daughter. Mine! Mine!

**STORYTELLER**
Mr. Akau, frustrated, looks around the room for a
way to escape. He stares into a large, ornate mirror—it's the Gouveias' mirror, the one that wit-
nessed the entire tragedy of the past. In this mirror, the Gouveias' tragedy is replayed for Mr.
Akau: the chaos, the curse, Mr. Gouveia tossing
the sacred staff out the house and into the heavy
brush below.

Mr. Akau is desperate to free himself, his legs still
held by some evil force. With a mighty pull, he
grabs the railing of the stairs and forces his legs
free. With his strong arms he catapults himself
out the nearest window. The house is swaying
from side to side. He sees his daughter's room
vibrating blue lights, like a strobe flashing, a
room about to explode. He runs deliriously, a
mad man sprinting into the woods.

**MRS. AKAU**
(*screaming at ghost*) Monster! You
want to fight? I'm not going down
without a fight. You want trouble?
I give you trouble!

## LEILANI/JUNIOR

Help! Daddy! Mommy! We're getting sucked into the mirror!

## STORYTELLER

Mrs. Akau dives for the bed—then all three are swirling above the ground, with Leilani half in the mirror. The roar gets louder. Mrs. Akau puts her legs on both sides of the mirror, struggling to free Leilani. Junior is fighting off the ghost with his toy sword. A piercing scream erupts in the room. Mr. Akau stands at the foot of the doorway—he is bleeding from diving out the glass window. With both arms outstretched, he lifts the sacred staff of the Kahuna, the only source that can save Mrs. Gouveia's spirit and set it free from the house to join the spirits of her family. The staff in Mr. Akau's hands starts to change, transforming into the head of the Kahuna.

## MR. AKAU

(*to the ghost*) Is this what you want? Will this set you free? The Kahuna?

## KAHUNA

You have suffered enough. Now you can join your family in the spiritual world. Go in peace. *Aloha.*

**MRS. GOUVEIA (ghost)**
Yes! Yes! Thank you! *Mahalo*.

**SON & DAUGHTER GOUVEIA (ghosts)**
Mommy! We're free. We're here.
We'll never leave you again!

**STORYTELLER**
Suddenly, all the noise stops. Furniture falls to
the floor. The rooms of the house look like a battle zone, and the Akaus all scramble to hug each
other. Bruised and exhausted, Junior breaks the
silence.

**AKAU, JR.**
Wow. Is this a great house or what,
Ma? Hey, Dad, we should do this
more often. This is better than
bowling.

**MR. AKAU**
Junior! You going get it this time.
Come here!

**STORYTELLER**

Laughing, Mrs. Akau and Leilani hug each other
as a new chase begins: Mr. Akau chasing Junior
around the room.

# The Pali

## CHARACTERS
Storyteller

Doris
Pam
Old Man

## SPECIAL EFFECTS (EFX)
*Wind blowing*
*Sound of car*
*Trees snapping*
*Car bumping*
*Crashing sounds*
*Car door creaking*
*Devilish laughter*

# STORYTELLER

The Pali. Legend has it that here, high above the Ko'olau Mountains, King Kamehameha's battle ended when hundreds of Hawaiian warriors retreated over the edge of the *pali* and were sent to their deaths. It is here that tourists and locals have seen unexplainable things. Locals would hesitate to take the drive from Honolulu to Kane'ohe. Sometimes cars carrying pork would sputter and die until the meat was tossed out. There were also some mysterious deaths.

But let's not dwell on the past and its dismal misgivings. Tonight is a new night; the air is thick with the fragrance of Hawai'i's tropical flowers and the moon is deathly white. Doris and Pam are driving alone after leaving a downtown party at Aloha Tower. They dread the thought of having to cross the Pali, especially when it's close to midnight.

Pam is a tall, sensitive Chinese girl who dwells on superstitions and taboos. Her friend, Doris, is the opposite. She is the sensible one, all business, but very caring. Doris loves people, all people. Well, almost.

The night is pitch black and the road ahead is spot-lighted by the car's headlights. The wind becomes fierce as they head up the mountain; the windshield of the car is slapped with leaves and squashed bugs. Suddenly, out of nowhere, a figure is seen hitchhiking. An old man, waving his hand, looks like he has an emergency. He's flagging for a ride. Pam and Doris don't see him yet; they're deep in conversation.

**DORIS**
Geez, you believe anything, eh, you?

**PAM**
Not everything. But sometimes, they say, when you go up the Pali for be careful. Last time my boyfriend went up, he took some pork. So when his car went stall, he went throw out the pork to get the car started. Scary, man.

**DORIS**

Well, we no more pork. Hey, maybe
your boyfriend should take some
pork and beans. Then maybe he no
need no car. Just skates, and toot
his way back to Kane'ohe.

*(The two girls scream with laughter)*

**DORIS**

Hey, stay real dark, man. What time
now?

**PAM**

(*excited*) Twelve o'clock midnight
already. Hurry up. We gotta go past
the Pali.

**DORIS**

Man, what a scarecrow.

**《◆EFX◆》**

*Wind blowing. Sound of the car.*

**DORIS**

(*surprised*) Hey, look. One old man
flagging us down.

**PAM**

(*scared*) No stop. I telling you. No
stop!

**DORIS**

What? That's just an old man.
Come on. We got to help him. He
might be sick.

**PAM**

Okay, but you going be sorry. I no
kid you.

**STORYTELLER**

Doris slows down the car to a halt. Pam is rolling
the window down so they can talk to him. Pam
notices the heavy wrinkles and his thick, spiny
white hair with a New York Yankees baseball cap
on his head. The old man leans forward to get
closer to talk as Pam is moving slowly away.
She's afraid to touch him. Doris is smiling.

**OLD MAN**

My wife—she's sick. She inside my
car. No can move her myself. I too
old. Help me. Please, help me.

**PAM**

(*to Doris*) No go! No go, Doris.  He
coming closer.

**STORYTELLER**

The old man stares at Doris and looks at Pam
with a grave feeling of desperation. He is soaked,
maybe from sweat, or a sudden rainfall. His smell
is different from anything Pam has ever come
across before, and he has long yellow teeth which
almost reveal their roots in his old age. He could
be ninety, or more.

**DORIS**

Shh! He going hear you. Old man,
where your car stay?

**OLD MAN**

Up the hill, not too far, on the Pali.

**PAM**

The Pali? Oh, we going get it now.

**DORIS**

Okay. Jump in the back seat. I help
you.

**PAM**

Doris, you're really nuts, man!

**STORYTELLER**

The old man struggles to open the door and
Doris reaches over to pull up the lock. Pam's eyes
are glued towards the road. She doesn't want any
part of this. All she wants is to get out of here and
get home.

**PAM**

(*to herself*) Why me? Why me?

**DORIS**

(*whispering*) Shut up, Pam! Come
inside, old man. I take you to the
Pali.

**OLD MAN**

*Mahalo.* I no forget you for this.

**PAM**

(*to herself*) I'll bet. We won't forget
this either.

**DORIS**

Quiet!

**STORYTELLER**

The old man slips into the back seat. Doris watches him in her rearview mirror. Pam has both of her arms stiffly crossed on her chest, eyes closed, saying prayers. Doris starts the car and proceeds to the Pali. As she reaches the Pali, she stops the car. The engine stops just before Doris turns off the ignition. She thinks nothing of it. She looks in the rearview mirror.

**DORIS**
> Where's your car, old man? We're
> on the Pali.

**⟪▸EFX◂⟫**
*Wind blowing. Trees snapping.*

**STORYTELLER**

The car rocks hard in the fierce winds of the Pali. Trees and branches are crashing about and whipping the car. Suddenly, the radio is silent, and the car lights shut off.

**PAM**
> He not there! He no stay!

**DORIS**
> How he went out? I never see him
> leave. Where is he? (*shouts*) Old
> man! Where are you?

## PAM

I told you. You no like listen.
C'mon, we go. We go! Let's get out
of here. Now!

## STORYTELLER

The car jerks from side to side, is lifted and
dropped, lifted, and dropped again. Doris grabs
the keys and tries to restart the car, panicking. A
glow of light outside the car encircles Pam and
Doris as they look out.

### (((▸EFX◂)))

*Wind blowing. Car bumping.*

## DORIS

I no can start the car. How come?
The key no fit! Help me, Pam, help
me.

## PAM

Look! He's in front of the car. He's
glowing in the dark. Geez. What is
this? What is happening?

### (((▸EFX◂)))

*Wild winds, crashing sounds against
the car.*

**DORIS**

(*panicked*) He's looking at me. He's looking at me! Help me! Help me start this car!

**STORYTELLER**

The glow of the old man starts moving toward Doris. Doris is hysterical and clumsy, trying to get the keys into the ignition. Each time the keys are near the ignition, they fall to the floor. Frustrated, she feels a cold sweat grab her like a steel claw. Her hair is tangled with sweat and confusion. She tries one more time to start the car. Nothing. She looks up in panic and gasps.

**PAM**

Doris, he's trying to get in. He's trying to open the door.

**⟪▸EFX◂⟫**

*Car door creaking. Wind thrashing.*

**DORIS**

I can't lock the door! What you want, old man? What?

**PAM**

His hand's coming through the glass! Doris, watch out!

**STORYTELLER**

Doris lets out a deathly scream. She imagines the old man's hands growing larger and larger. In his hands is a heavy rope and he places it around her neck like a hangman's noose. Pam watches in horror as the car lights up brightly, intensely, from the inside. The car seems to lift off the ground, then slams down on the ground again, then spins as if it's out of control.

**DORIS**
> I feel his hands on me. Let go—
> (*calmer*) I feel his hands on me.

**STORYTELLER**

Doris' fear has gone. Doris looks around and everything is calm, untouched. The interior lights pop on and Pam is looking at Doris, her eyes bugging out of her head. Pam touches Doris' shoulder as Doris, still dumbfounded, stares at the lights on the dashboard.

**PAM**
> He touched you. I saw him. He touched you. You okay, Doris? You okay?

### DORIS

(*calm*) I feel good. So... alive. I
never felt like this before. How
come I feel like this?

### PAM

I think because you went stop and
help him, he thanked you the only
way he could.

### DORIS

We so stupid. We get all scared for
nothing. We imagined all this madness. He was just an old man. All
our hang-ups, that's why. That's
why we screamed. We never try to
understand his kindness.

### PAM

Especially me, man. (*pause*) Gee,
you smell good, too. What's that
smell?

### DORIS

(*startled*) Gardenia! He put one gardenia lei around my neck. I thought
it was a rope. I'm so insecure. Hey, I
believe in ghosts. I really believe.

**PAM**

You can say that again. Boy, you can
say that anytime.

**STORYTELLER**

So what seemed to be a horrific event wasn't really an event after all, just the minds of two young
girls driven to believe the unnatural nature of
things as evil. But it wasn't, was it? There will
always be two sides of looking at things. It's really
what you want to believe, right?

**⟨⟨►EFX◄⟩⟩**

*Devilish laughter. The wind erupts
wildly again.*

# The Obake

## CHARACTERS
Storyteller

Mom
Dad
Rosy
Junior
Old Woman

## SPECIAL EFFECTS (EFX)
*Knocking on door*
*Scratching sounds*
*Door slamming*

# STORYTELLER

I t was my first trip to Maui and I had a chance to meet my cousin, Rosy, for the first time. We had always talked on the telephone, and at eight years old, I was on my way to my first adventure. My parents are from the old country, Japan, and I was raised with stories of the gallant *samurais*, the *geishas*, the Kabuki plays, and the Japanese Westerns which had swords instead of guns. Then, there was the *obake*.

The *obake*. The scariest of all the demons known to man. Scarier than Frankenstein, Dracula, even the Werewolf. Why? Because the *obake* was everything. It was never one thing. It could transform itself into any monster it wanted to be—or even not a monster, but a tiny bug or spider, an old man, old woman, anything. Anywhere.

We lived in Kane'ohe, and sometimes I would gaze out of my window and watch the blue skies against our majestic mountains, the Ko'olaus. The skies would play funny tricks on me. One time, a sudden roar of thunder and lightning crashed, sending tons of water down the Ko'olaus. The rain was so fierce that the waterfalls were like rivers coming down. And with another crash of lightning, the gushing waterfalls climbed back up to where they came from, up the mountain. This is the Hawai'i I remember.

Wait, Mom's calling.

**JUNIOR**

Yes, mom?

**STORYTELLER**

Gotta go. We've got to get ready for my cousin, Rosy, on Maui.

**DAD**

Junior, listen. Be sure you get everything in your bag, okay?

**MOM**

Yeah. Remember the *obake*.

**STORYTELLER**

See what I mean? Even mentioning the *obake* would scare us into being good. So I listened.

We drove to the Honolulu Airport. We didn't have jet planes then; we had a silver, two engine job that made a lot of noise, and made my legs cold. The stewardesses matched those DC-7s—not so pretty. They gave us Chicklets, a hard-coated gum that looked like green bathroom tile, to help your head clear when the plane climbed into the air.

As I looked out the round porthole to the approaching land, the island of Maui was like a dish, ready to be served. There were beautiful rolling hills, vast rich vegetation swelling up Haleakala. I thought that was where the *obakes* hung out; thought they were responsible for killing the now extinct volcano.

Driving to my cousin's plantation home, the dirt looked blood red with the rich green trees and hibiscus everywhere. The contrast was overwhelming. I never saw grass so green. Everything seemed magnified. Then I saw Rosy.

She was no great beauty. She was standing with her head cocked to her right shoulder, oversized glasses sliding down her small nose. She's my cousin, so I had to be nice. Funny how you imagine people look over the telephone. She wasn't what I'd imagined. She looked too, well, serious.

She was nice, though. She gave me a frog. Plenty of frogs in Maui. This one had a great smile. Then she took me down to the stream.

When we got back, my mom and dad and relatives decided we needed food. Old people always need food. They must have forgotten how much adventure there is around them, waiting. Who had time for food?

**MOM**

Okay, kids. We going shopping.
Daddy said no go play on the street
or you going get lickens. You stay in
the house and lock the door. You
remember the *obake* story, now.
You lock the door! No let nobody
in, okay, Rosy?

**ROSY**

Yes, Aunty.

**MOM**

Junior?

**JUNIOR**

(*giggling*) Yes, Mommy.

**DAD**

Junior, you listen now. Hear?

**JUNIOR**

I'll be good.

**MOM**

Okay, see you guys in one hour.
'Bye now.

**ROSY/JUNIOR**

Okay. Bye!

**STORYTELLER**

As my mother left with the rest of the family, we
were abandoned in this little house in the middle
of Maui, with nothing to protect me but my
cousin, Rosy. How was she going to protect me?
Her glasses were so thick that her eyes looked like
they were blown up. She looked like a goldfish in
a tank. And she was scared of everything. I
thought that I would have to take care of her,
even if she was two years older than I was. I heard
the car door slam, the engine start, and the only
means of escape now was departing with my
mom and dad. I decided to be brave.

**ROSY**

You have to laugh. Get *obake*, you
know. Mom always tells me about
the *obake*.

**JUNIOR**

Why, you see one, or what?

**ROSY**

No, but daddy said the *obake* can
look like anything. Can be one spider, one bird, can be an old man.
Anything. They like small kids like
us, too. They eat small kids.

**JUNIOR**

Oh, yeah? Well, I can beef 'em. I
can punch them in the stomach. I
no scared of the *obake*. The *obake*
going run away from me.

**ROSY**

Real tough. You wait. Someday you
going get it, tough guy. You watch,
big mouth. You better put your
things away like Aunty said.

**JUNIOR**

I going play with my frog.

**ROSY**

Junior, your mommy said—

((▶EFX◀))

*Knocking on door.*

**STORYTELLER**

We heard a knock. A slow, sinister knock. It came
from the back door, next to the kitchen. Rosy and
I looked at each other. We headed for the kitchen.
As we looked out the window, we saw an old
woman with a hunched back, dressed in old rags,
carrying a bag. It looked empty. She peeked inside
the house, searching to see if anyone was there.

((▶EFX◀))

*Knocking grows louder.*

**OLD WOMAN**

Keikis, keikis. Come to Aunty.
Open the door. I get plenty candy
for you. Open the door.

((▶EFX◀))

*Banging on door.*

**ROSY**

Junior!

**JUNIOR**

What? Who that?

**ROSY**

I don't know.

**JUNIOR**

Go see!

**ROSY**

Oh, no. Not me. You the tough guy.
You go.

**JUNIOR**

Okay. I'll go see. (*whispering*) Only
one old lady. I wonder what's in the
bag.

**STORYTELLER**

Junior walks slowly to the kitchen, barely looking
at the screen, not wanting to make eye contact
with the old woman. She shifts to get a better
look at Junior. Junior looks at her silver white
hair and notices all those wrinkles crammed on
her forehead. Her eyes pierce him like the two
eyes of a black rat. Her long fingers press against
the screen; her fingernails are long, unkempt.
She's scratching the door, trying to claw her way
in.

((►**EFX**◄))

*Scratching sounds.*

**JUNIOR**

(*tough talk*) What you like, old lady?

**STORYTELLER**

Rosy is behind the icebox, watching this surprise event, trying to see the old woman's face. She's trying not to be scared.

**OLD WOMAN**

(*sweet*) I get candy. You like candy? Tell your sister, too. I get plenty candy. No scared. Come to me, little boy.

**JUNIOR**

My mommy said to let nobody inside. Nobody.

**ROSY**

Yeah! We cannot go out. Go away! Go away!

**OLD WOMAN**

Open, children. I can play with you. Now!

## JUNIOR

No! Go away!

## ROSY

(*crying*) Go away! We going call the
police. Go away!

## JUNIOR

(*crying*) Go away!

## STORYTELLER

The old woman, impatient, bangs on the door.
Her eyes widen. Rosy quickly slips the latch on as
Junior grabs her hand to get out of the kitchen.
The old lady cuts the screen with her long fingernails and slips her hand in to pull up the latch.
The kids scurry away, listening as the sounds of
the old woman's voice turn into the screeching
sounds of a wild animal. They head for the back
room with the old lady right behind them, about
to jump on their backs. They reach the room in
time and grab the door quickly. It slams shut on
her hand.

*Door slamming.*

**ROSY**

Junior, she's trying to come in.
(*screams*) Her hand! Her hand—it's
changing.

**JUNIOR**

Slam the door on her hand again.
Quick! Slam the door on her...
claws!

**ROSY/JUNIOR**

Her hands changed to claws! She's
changed into a rat!

**OLD WOMAN**

(*screaming in pain*) Eeaaaccchhh!
You slammed the door on my
hand! I am going to eat you both
for dinner. Come now, children.

**STORYTELLER**

The old woman is now a raging rat, clawing her
way through the locked bedroom door. The
scratching becomes louder and we dive under the
bed, grabbing the bed legs to anchor us.

*Scratching sounds.*

**STORYTELLER**

My eyes look back from under the bed as the door is gnawed to pieces. The rat crashes through and grabs my ankles. Rosy is screaming, holding onto me and the bedpost. The rat is getting the bag with one hand and pulling with the other. Everything seems to be erupting. Suddenly, we hear the voices of my mom and dad.

**MOM/DAD**

Junior? Rosy? Hey guys, help us with the groceries. Where are you? Junior! Rosy!

**STORYTELLER**

I open my eyes, fearful, and look at Rosy. Her glasses are fogged up and her pupils are popping out at me. I am equally afraid. We yell for help. We run out of the bedroom like two wild young bats, not seeing that the door we thought was chewed by the large rat is actually normal. Not a scratch on it.

**MOM**

Are you guys happy to see me or
what? I'd be glad to see anybody
after seeing that big black rat running out of the kitchen.

**ROSY/JUNIOR**

(*laughing and crying*) We missed
you! We love you.

**MOM**

Missed me and love me, huh?

**ROSY/JUNIOR**

Yes. Now we believe in *obakes*.

**MOM**

*Obakes*? Hmmm.

**STORYTELLER**

Was it just a figment of our young minds? Or was it the mystique of the *obake*'s evil ways? How could everything be untouched, as if nothing had happened? The screen door was untouched. The bedroom door, too.

And how could two people be engaged in such terror and at the same time still be able to talk about it as if it were yesterday: fresh, clear, horrifying. You be the judge.

Do I believe in *obakes*? You bet your sweet *okole* I do.

# Nu'uanu Cemetery

## CHARACTERS
Storyteller

Mom
Dad
Shirley
Gino
Gladys
Ghosts

## SPECIAL EFFECTS (EFX)
*Crash of lightning*
*Wind blowing*
*Ghosts cry out*
*Trees/branches crashing*
*Loud screams*

# STORYTELLER

**D**o you know fear?

I'm fifty-seven years old and people who know me say that I have it all. I have a beautiful, loving wife; a handsome son who bears my name; and a big, comfortable home. I'm successful as an artist, and my career takes me everywhere. I have good health, played football—was even a cop once. But when someone asks me what my biggest fear is, I tell them: "Fishies."

That's right. Tiny gold fishies that swim around in streams, that nibble on white bread. This is the story of those tiny fishies that keep me from ever growing old. Because at fifty-seven I can remember myself at seven years old, cupping those fish in my hands as all craziness broke loose around me at Nu'uanu Cemetery.

It is 7:30 a.m. A school day. My name is Gino. My sister and I are seated, having breakfast. My sister's name is Shirley. She's nine years old and I, her only brother, am trying to hurry and gulp my breakfast so I can get down to business. The business that I have in mind is fishing. It's Tuesday. It's piano lesson day, and it's fish day.

Nuʻuanu Cemetery. The very thought can conjure up my childhood as if I had just turned around a corner. The bright, beautiful blue skies, the greenness of the valley, the lush wonderful aroma that permeates my home, Hawaiʻi. Nuʻuanu's bright side is all that and more. The little town brings back thoughts of *saimin*, guava jam, *manapua* and coconut candy. The happy people would stop and talk to you. People knew how to talk back then. I always said "Hello" to Gladys, who sold bright red apples from *Wah-shing-ton*. She taught me that: *Wah-shing-ton* apples. Big, fat, juicy apples, growing larger with each bite. I can hear her now.

### GLADYS
Gino! You going eat that big apple,
or what? Your hand too small. Let
me get you one small one, okay?

### GINO
No.

### GLADYS
Okay. You like be one big palooka
like your Papa, eh?

### GINO
Yes!

**STORYTELLER**

Like I said, I mean, we talked. She was very old,
and she had strange marks on her hands. They
were blue and black and were on her knuckles. I
later found out that she was from *Oh-kee-nah-
wah*. She taught me that, too. She was one nice
lady.

**DAD**

Gino, sit down and finish your
toast.

**GINO**

(*excited*) I have to go, Daddy. I
going be late.

**SHIRLEY**

He just want to find one bottle for
the fishies.

**MOM**

What fish?

**SHIRLEY**

After piano lessons, we going down
the stream to catch fish. Gino catch
two already.

**GINO**

Mommy, buy me one fish tank. I
take care of the fishies. Please?
Mommy, please?

**MOM**

(*stern*) No. I don't want fish here.
You stealing baby fish from their
mothers. You no shame? The baby
fish need their mommies too, you
know.

**GINO**

Aw, Mom.

**DAD**

You better listen to your Mom,
Gino. Hurry up. Get your books.
Late already.

**MOM**

And don't forget your lunch. You
always forget your lunch. Shirley!
Get his lunch.

**DAD**

Shirley, Gino, come here.

**SHIRLEY/GINO**

Yes, Daddy?

**DAD**

You listen to your Mommy. No
catch fish.

**SHIRLEY/GINO**

Yes, Daddy. We come straight
home.

**MOM**

You promise?

**SHIRLEY/GINO**

Yes, Mommy. We promise.

**MOM**

By the time you finish piano
lessons, going be 4:30. Getting
dark. I don't want to hear you going
down to the cemetery that late, you
hear? Sun going down fast, you
know. The cemetery really scary.

**SHIRLEY/GINO**

We come right home.

**MOM**

Daddy, you too. Come right home.
And no forget your lunch.

## STORYTELLER

We all scramble to get out of the house. It's always a cat and mouse game, Shirley running into me, Dad tripping over my books. Mom stands and watches. She always shakes her head and goes back to the kitchen, hands thrown up in defeat.

Shirley and I went to a public school near our home but when school was out, we headed to a Catholic convent to take our piano lessons every Tuesday and Thursday. Why was I taking piano lessons? These hands were for catching fishies. Unlike me, my sister was preparing to be a concert pianist. She was constantly doing scales; her metronome was a part of her anatomy. Tick-tock, tick-tock. She was like a machine. But me— I couldn't see anything but fishies looking at me, their big, buggy eyes in my mayonnaise jar.

I still remember the convent propped above the cemetery. Sometimes, when we were late, we'd take the shortcut and walk through the cemetery to the stream, then up to the convent. Every trip was an adventure. There were jaguars, lions and alligators, and the papaya trees looked like the long necks of giraffes peering over the trees. The large smooth rocks around the stream were giant turtles that moved at zero miles per hour...

**SHIRLEY**

Hurry up, stupid! Getting late. We
got to get to class. Sister going be
mad. Hurry, slow poke. Stop
dreaming!

**STORYTELLER**

My sister, Shirley. Piano, piano, piano. No life.
Then, there was Sister Marie Henriette, the
scourge of Notre Dame, the master of disaster.
"Zorro" in black on black. Her stiff, starched
white crinoline ruffle surrounded her round face.
She never smiled, and she had a stick attached to
her hand that never stopped striking things: me,
the piano, me, the piano keys, me, my *okole*.

But wait! Once I caught her smile. I memorized
my lessons because of that infernal stick. When
she told me to begin, I completed the entire rou-
tine perfectly. True blue. I looked up at her,
proud. And you know what? She hadn't even
opened the book yet. I waited for the hit. I gri-
maced and pressed my hands hard on the keys as
she—guess what?—grabbed me and kissed me.

Even so, waiting to finish class was like eternity.
The clang of the bell was like a shot out of a cannon. Grabbing my books, I rushed down to the
cafeteria, hoping to find a mayonnaise bottle in
the trash.

And there it was. Shiny and clean, waiting for Gino. I grabbed it and ran for Shirley. Time to fish.

Shirley, however, was not happy to see that bottle.

### SHIRLEY
What did Daddy say? No fishing!
You crazy? We going get lickens.

### GINO
Aw, Shirley. Just one. Just one. Well,
two. One for you, okay? Two. Just
two.

### SHIRLEY
It's already 4:30. The sun going
down already. We'll be late for dinner.

### GINO
Okay, you go. I'll stay. I can fish by
myself.

### STORYTELLER
And I meant every word of it. I could. So I started
down the stream. I took a sly look back at Shirley
standing there, mad as heck. She grabbed her
books and followed me to the stream. She knew
that she couldn't go home without me.

**SHIRLEY**

Okay, okay. Make it fast. We had it, anyway.

**STORYTELLER**

So we did. My mayonnaise bottle was a bottle no longer, but a basket of bait and hooks and flies. I took my shoes off, rolled up my pants and sleeves so I could reach down, deep into their hiding places. I was now... a great explorer in Africa.

**GINO**

Wait. I see one. It's red. I see one.

**SHIRLEY**

Gino, be careful. Don't go too deep! Gino!

**STORYTELLER**

Suddenly in one terrifying moment, it was as if this was happening to someone else.

**GINO**

(*screams*) What was that? There's something else in here. Help, Shirley!

**(((▸EFX◂)))**

*Crash of lightning. Whooshing wind. Ghosts cry out.*

**STORYTELLER**

Gino is pulled into the stream. Shirley rushes to try and save him. Then, an ugly crash of lightning is heard, followed by thunderous sounds. A large tree snaps and falls between Shirley and Gino. Shirley reaches toward Gino while her legs and other hand grasp the fallen tree. As their hands get closer, another crash of lightning is seen—a flash warning that travels instantly to Mom.

It begins to rain furiously. Mom, preparing dinner, turns to the flash. Startled, she drops a glass and cuts herself. She suddenly knows that something is terribly wrong, and it's happening this moment. The kitchen window is hammered by a branch outside, and the wind is screaming Gino's voice.

**((▸EFX◂))**
*Wind howling. Branches snapping.*

**GINO**
Help me, Mommy. Help me!

**MOM**
Gino! Shirley!

## STORYTELLER

She panics. She forgets her shoes, her umbrella. She heads for the sound in the violent wind. She is wondering where they could possibly be. She raises her arms and tries to feel her children. The rain tears at her face, stinging with every drop. She is pulled instinctively, and runs hard now. The wind and rain are pounding, unrelentless. Every step is difficult. Every step, eternity. Her only thought is the stream below their house. That stream belongs to Nu'uanu Cemetery, to the dead people who make it their permanent home. She knows that someone has intruded their sacred ground, and they are punishing those that dare to intrude. What she does not know is that the intruder is her son.

### ((▸EFX◂))
*Lightning. Ghosts howl and cry out.*

## STORYTELLER

There is a red glow up ahead. The stream is near-by. The trees are bending at such an angle that it's a wonder they're still standing. She spots Shirley hanging onto a fallen tree. Running and falling, her hands and feet are torn by branches and loose rocks. The glow becomes brighter, the howling louder. Gino barely hangs on—ghostly figures are trying to take him with them into the stream.

**SHIRLEY**

Mommy! Help us! I cannot hold
on much longer.

**MOM**

Hold on! Never let go! I'm coming!
Hold on, Gino.

**GINO**

Mommy! I'm sorry! It's my fault!

**MOM**

Be quiet and hold on!

**STORYTELLER**

The stream is violent with water and branches fly-
ing everywhere. Gino is losing his grip. Shirley
can barely hang on to him, and Mom is still too
far away. She stops and looks to the skies.

**GHOSTS**

We want him. We want him.

**MOM**

No! You can't have him!

**STORYTELLER**

Mom is angry. She puts her fist to the evil spirits and demands they free her child. She points her finger in defiance, commanding them to stop. Then, she pleads with God to help her.

**MOM**

God, is this what you planned? To give my son to the devil? Is this what you want? Help me! They are trying to take my kids!

**STORYTELLER**

Nothing. The onslaught continues in a crescendo of thunderous disapproval.

**MOM**

God! Is this your plan? Don't leave me now. You are my only hope. Now, please! Help me now!

**STORYTELLER**

Suddenly the opposing force is attacked by a crashing sound behind her, switching the direction of the wind and rain against the evil force in front of her. The trees are slapping the red glow. Rocks and water are tearing into the evil's rage. Then, the voice of the devil is heard.

((►**EFX**◄))
*Loud screams, getting gradually softer.*

**STORYTELLER**

Mom is by Shirley's side. They both strain to hold Gino. The force becomes weaker; then, they both fall backwards as it releases them. Everything stops. They both lay on the ground, breathing heavily.

Suddenly, they are both blinded by the sun. The clouds move swiftly away. Then they see Gino, above them, clothes ripped to shreds, bloodied and bruised.

**GINO**

(*awestruck*) Miracle Mom! (*giggles*) What took you so long?

**MOM**

Gino!

**STORYTELLER**

The three fall together and begin wrestling, hugging, covering themselves with leaves and mud.

# Ni'ihau, the Last Banzai

## CHARACTERS

Storyteller

Colonel Seichi Toguchi
Kahuna
Soldier

## SPECIAL EFFECTS (EFX)

*Explosions*
*Sound of airplane*
*Gunfire*
*Sputtering engine*
*Howling wind*
*Airplane crashing*

# STORYTELLER

**D**ecember 7, 1941. Approximately 7:22 a.m. Colonel Seichi Toguchi is leading his squadron of fighter pilots towards Pearl Harbor. He is with the second wave of pilots to hit Pearl Harbor on this black day that marks the beginning of World War II.

The sky is scarred with cannon explosions and high caliber tracers. The ground is spotty with smoke trails and mangled machinery. Ships are on fire and exploding right there, where they are anchored.

Colonel Toguchi is one of the Imperial Japanese Navy, a loyal soldier, and a devoted family man. A family photo has been placed where his eyes can easily find it. This photo—picturing his wife, Nachang; his daughter, Fuchang; and his young son, Yukio—was blessed along with his trusty *samurai* fighting sword, the mark of a true descendent of the *samurais*, leaders and warriors of old Japan. Although he has fought in other wars, he has never understood why men must harm each other. All he ever wanted was to be home with his wife and family, in peace, raising his young ones and enjoying his one passion, botany.

In an instant, he enters a dive. He aims his plane towards a large building on Hickam Air Force Base.

*Explosion, sound of aircraft.*

## STORYTELLER

He unloads a couple of bombs and, just as quickly, pulls his plane upwards, hearing the roar of explosions behind him. Direct hits. He tilts his wings to view the damage, but his plane is suddenly rocked with heavy artillery, ripping his aircraft with baseball-sized bullets and shrapnel from one wing to another. The force of the bullets punch gaping holes as they rip through the aircraft.

(((►EFX◄)))
*Gunfire. Explosions.*

## STORYTELLER

More large fifty caliber bullet heads tear through his instrument panel and in a painful shock, tear the tip of his left shoe off, severing some of his toes. More shrapnel grazes his collar bone, narrowly missing his head. The cockpit is engulfed in smoke. His altimeter is broken and his plane sputters, gradually losing altitude. He forces his window back with his strong arm to let the smoke out and to unload the burning smoke from his lungs. Fresh air gushes in, clearing his mind and bringing him back to consciousness.

Breathing hard and trying to stay in control, he channels his plane out to sea, due north, away from this madness, this unholy war. He holds his plane steady, out to the last main island of the Hawaiian chain: Ni'ihau. His emergency calls may be sent out, but they may not be received. He radios that he is headed towards Ni'ihau and will crash land on the first clearing available. He prays that his radio is working. He prays that he will see his sweet family once again.

He is numbed by the chaos. His shoulder is throbbing, and the pain in his foot is excruciating. In his mind, all that remains of his foot is a stump. The cold air whipping into his boot is more than he can stand. With his right hand, he pulls his thick white scarf off and forces his arm to reach his tortured foot. There, he feels a good part of his foot still intact.

### COLONEL TOGUCHI
(*in pain*) Please help me get this scarf on my foot. The pain! This awful pain. (*a grave laugh*) Well, at least I still have most of my foot. One and three-quarters foot is better than nothing.

((▸**EFX**◂))

*Sputtering engine. The wind howls.*

**STORYTELLER**

Trying to maintain control, Toguchi concentrates on his shoulder wound. He sees blood covering the patch that bears the Japanese flag of the Rising Sun, and he thinks that is a bad omen. He takes a deep breath to avoid unconsciousness. He screams to stay alive. He cries out for his wife and kids.

**COLONEL TOGUCHI**

Nachang! Fuchang! Yukio! I want to live. I do not want to fight any-more! I promise you, I will not die. I will not leave you! I will not aban-don you.

**STORYTELLER**

Semi-delirious, he sights land. He flies slowly, just above the coconut trees. Carefully, he levels his craft and aims for the first narrow strip of heavy brush.

((▸**EFX**◂))

*Crashing sounds.*

**STORYTELLER**

He is coming down with such force that tree tops are chopped away easily. He lands with such impact that the plane acts as a giant lawn mower, leaving a jagged path of downed trees and grass in its wake. The plane digs into the ground, careens up a slight hill, then slams to a solid stop. A small fire erupts. Sparks from the electrical wires of the instrument panel start to pop.

**COLONEL TOGUCHI**

(*delirious*) I've got to get out. It's going to blow.  Help me get out of this seat. (*screaming*) My foot! My shoulder! I hate this war!

**STORYTELLER**

Halfway out of the cockpit, he reaches for his family's picture and grabs his service revolver. He flips backward and falls heavily on the wing and down towards the bottom of a small ravine. He watches as the plane is engulfed in flames. He digs into the ground with all the energy he has left, and then moves forward, slowly, toward safety.

**《▶EFX◀》**

*KABOOM! Explosion.*

## STORYTELLER

Partly unconscious, he is awakened by his pain. He unbuckles his parachute and lifts his goggles gingerly to his forehead. His eyes are burning from smoke and grease. His mind is blurred. Panicking, he sees a figure in front of him, a man trying to reach for him. Colonel Toguchi, delirious, screams at the man. Of all his experiences, he has never known fear like this—this unbearable, this excruciating. He warns the stranger to stay back.

### COLONEL TOGUCHI
> Stay away! Please, I do not want to hurt you. Don't make me use this gun. Stay away, I'm warning you!

### STORYTELLER

Colonel Toguchi fires out of sheer anxiety. Two shots ring out. The Colonel does not know that he has just shot a sacred Hawaiian priest, a Kahuna. The Kahuna falls back, seemingly dead.

### COLONEL TOGUCHI
> Why did you make me shoot you? I warned you. I don't know who you are.

## STORYTELLER

The Colonel is shaking, looking at the Kahuna. Just then, the Kahuna slowly opens his eyes, stares at the Colonel, and stands up again. He walks toward the Colonel with arms outstretched, still wanting to help the Colonel. The Colonel can't believe his eyes. This person has taken two direct hits to the heart and is still alive. The Kahuna still walks toward the Colonel. The Colonel is stunned. He finally faints from complete shock.

Unconscious, Colonel Toguchi falls into a deep coma. In the coma, a nightmare begins to unravel. He is trapped beyond the threshold of his deepest depression where reality has disappeared. He is witnessing firsthand the transformation of his body. In the dream, he sees his innermost conflicts and fears. His body is being dissected; his insides emerge and he watches them float slowly outside of his body. His eyes turn inward to observe the confines of his brain. He witnesses all this and suddenly understands the substance that he is made from. He is ashamed of what he finds. He wants to escape this nightmare. He screams.

He wakes in a small shack. The man who he shot is tending to his wounds. Their only means of communication is broken English. Slowly, they begin to understand each other.

**COLONEL TOGUCHI**

Who are you? What are you doing?
Where am I?

**KAHUNA**

I am a priest. My people call me
Kahuna. You were hurt and I came
to help you.

**COLONEL TOGUCHI**

I'm sorry. I'm sorry, please! I was
confused. I'm sorry I shot you.

**KAHUNA**

You didn't shoot me. You just had a
bad dream. You were very, very sick.

**COLONEL TOGUCHI**

So sorry. I was scared. Please,
please. I wish I could change things.

**KAHUNA**

You, soldier— you should learn not
to hurt people. Be good to everyone.

**COLONEL TOGUCHI**

(*calling for his family*) Nachang!
Fuchang! Yukio! Forgive your
father. I am just a soldier, ordered
to hurt people. Kahuna, I am not a
killer. I love people. Please understand, Kahuna. I hate to kill anybody.

**STORYTELLER**

The Colonel slips into a deep sleep. Exhaustion
and depression set in. He shivers like a tormented
animal. He is slowly slipping away, slowly resign-
ing himself to death. He regrets he ever existed.

The Kahuna notices this and tries frantically to
save this Colonel, this family man. He was only
following the orders of his superiors. He forgives
the Colonel with his own prayers and the gods of
Hawai'i respond by returning to him his life's
breath, strengthening him back to health.

The Colonel awakens in shock, calling for his
wife. The Kahuna is busy pressing herbs and oils
into his wounds, wrapping his shoulder with ti
leaves and clean cloth. His foot is completely
bandaged with heavy gauze and herbal medicine.
The pain has ceased. The Colonel watches the
Kahuna carefully tend to his wounds while hum-
ming an old Hawaiian tune, soothing the pain

and regaining the spirits of humanity. The Colonel tries to sit up, not realizing that he has been unconscious for two weeks. He asks the Kahuna what happened.

### KAHUNA
You are in my *hale*, my house. I am the Kahuna, the priest of this village, and you have been very sick. Now I think you will live.

### COLONEL TOGUCHI
But I saw myself open up. I saw my insides. How come I see that?

### KAHUNA
We want you to see the real you. When you see inside yourself, that you can understand yourself.

### COLONEL TOGUCHI
(*confused*) But why you keep me alive? Why you let me live? I am bad.

### KAHUNA
The gods and I see you innocent. We feel your great love for your children and wife. We no kill you.

**COLONEL TOGUCHI**
Oh, thank you, Kahuna. I am so
sorry.

**STORYTELLER**
Suddenly the Kahuna's home is invaded by
Japanese soldiers trying to rescue their comrade.
Being soldiers, they are brusque and cruel to
everyone. They gather a group of Hawaiians for
an immediate retaliation.

**SOLDIER**
Colonel, sir, we are here to rescue
you and take you back to the fleet.
I will show our enemies that we
mean business. Then we'll go. Burn
up the village, men.

**COLONEL TOGUCHI**
Idiots! Stop this craziness. No
more. These people helped me stay
alive. They helped me be whole
again, to see my family. Enough!

**STORYTELLER**
The Colonel stands. He gingerly puts on his uni-
form and reaches for his cap. The Kahuna hands
him photos of his family and tells him to go in
peace.

**KAHUNA**

Colonel, remember, the world is
full of good people like yourself.
Be good to all.

**COLONEL TOGUCHI**

*Hai*, Kahuna. *Arigato gozaimasu*,
Kahuna. *Banzai! Banzai! Banzai!*

**STORYTELLER**

The Colonel looks from the Hawaiians gathered
to the Kahuna and bows. With gratitude, he
leaves his family's highest honor—the family
sword of the *samurai*—and orders his troops to
bow to the people of Hawai'i in respect for the
Kahuna and their gods.

*PAU*
(FINISHED)

# Other chapter book favorites from
# The Adventures in Hawaii Series

### Makoa and The Place of Refuge

Written by Jerry Cunnyngham
Illustrated by Sharon Alshams

*Makoa is running for his life!...* This tale of old Hawaii is about a young boy, Makoa, who has broken a great *kapu* which condemns him to death. Can he reach Pu'uhonua o Honaunau (the Place of Refuge) before his pursuers put a spear through his heart?

### The Microchip Caper

Written by Robert Graham
Illustrated by Sharon Alshams

Julie and Todd have sailed with their parents and their pet parrot from California to Hawaii. In Honolulu, they became friends with Moana and Kai. The new friends are soon creeping onto a strange boat in the middle of the night as they try to solve the mystery of *The Microchip Caper.*

### The Thief in Chinatown

Written by Elaine Masters
Illustrated by Sharon Alshams

There is big trouble in Honolulu's Chinatown in 1896! Six oranges have been stolen from Wong's Grocery. The thief turns out to be a runaway boy from a ship in the harbor. Excitement builds as the Wong family tries to hide and protect the boy who stole their oranges.

### Surfer Boy

Written by gaël Mustapha
Illustrated by Ron Croci

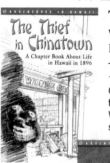

*Surfer Boy* chronicles the contemporary story of a 15-year old boy who lives in Laie on the island of Oahu. The story focus is on surfing, getting a driver's license, first love, family relationships, and friendships.